COOKED AND BOOKED

RAISED AND GLAZED COZY MYSTERIES,
BOOK 32

EMMA AINSLEY

SUMMER PRESCOTT BOOKS PUBLISHING

CHAPTER ONE

"I don't understand why I can't have one of those myself." Orson Hawley hovered over the platter of warm donuts and frowned. Despite his age, Orson's expression bore a striking resemblance to his adopted grandchildren's faces when they were told "no" by one of their parents.

"I don't know how many times I'm going to have to explain this," Maggie Mission, owner of Dogwood Donuts, said. "These donuts are for display purposes only. Ruby is about to host a book signing for her latest cookbook. You know that. I've already told you that if you want one of the donuts, you are more than welcome to go into the kitchen and get one for yourself."

"Why do I have to go all the way back in the

kitchen for a donut?" Orson argued. "I don't work for you anymore. I'm a paying customer and I want a donut."

Maggie couldn't help herself. She broke into laughter at Orson's comment. "I don't think you've paid for a single donut since I inherited this donut shop from my Aunt Marjorie. And you certainly haven't paid for a donut since you came to work for me. Even in retirement, you're still not a paying customer, but, if you'll give me a minute, I'll go back there and get a donut for you. Just keep your hands out of these!"

Although her own son Bradley was a full-grown adult and a father himself, she often felt like she was dealing with a child when Orson was around.

"Why is Ruby having a book signing here, anyway?" Orson grumbled. He sat back down at the Old Timer's table and crossed his arms. "Why isn't she down in Little Rock or something, like usual?"

Maggie slowly exhaled and retied her apron around her waist. She was determined to keep her nice clothes clean for the book signing. "Because, like I've told you before, her editor decided featuring her latest baking cookbook here was a good idea," Maggie said. "It has something to do with Ruby being part owner of the business. I'm not sure I understand how publishing works, but this is what we're doing. Now please, stay out of the donuts."

"I wouldn't be a threat to these donuts if you would just hurry back into the kitchen and get me one of my own." Orson raised his eyes to her and grinned like he had just solved the world's most pressing problem.

"Fine," Maggie said. "I'll go get you a donut, but please, stay out of the way while everyone arrives. We're about to have the dining room filled with people wanting an autographed copy of the cookbook."

"You hope," Orson said.

"What does that mean?" Maggie asked. She made it as far as the counter and turned to look back at him.

Orson shrugged innocently. "I just mean that you always hope people turn up for a book signing, but there's never a guarantee that very many people will show up. Right?" He tossed the question across the room at Ruby who was nervously shuffling around freshly printed copies of her cookbook.

"Technically, that's right, but just so you know, even if no one else shows up, you still can't have those donuts." Ruby cracked a smile.

Maggie bit her bottom lip to keep the laughter inside. She decided not to stoke Orson's fire any further by laughing at Ruby's response. Instead, she pushed through the swinging door that led into the kitchen and made her way to the cooling rack where the fresh, black walnut and apple donuts cooled.

"Have you had one of these yet?" Naomi Gardner asked. She rested against the sink with a donut in her hand. "Ruby has really outdone herself once again."

"I sampled one when she was coming up with the recipe," Maggie admitted. She pulled a white ceramic saucer from the shelf in the storage room and carried it over to the cooling rack. "I haven't tried one of these yet, though."

"Oh, you really should," Naomi said. "I mean, just the way she arranges these things is a work of art." Naomi turned the donut over in her hand. It was a simple cake batter donut recipe, with raw apple chunks and roasted Ozark black walnuts in the batter. Ruby had chosen a black walnut and caramel icing that she dipped only half of the donut in, followed by a generous sprinkling of cinnamon and sugar all the way around. Naomi was right. There was more than just the wonderful taste to the donuts. The appearance was pleasant to the eye.

"Have people begun to arrive yet?" Myra Sawyer Macklin called out to her from the office. Naomi and Myra were two of the donut shops most faithful employees, not to mention dear friends. It was Myra's daughter that Orson, who lived with her and her husband Brooks, most resembled when he took to pouting.

"Not yet." Maggie plucked two fresh donuts off the rack and arranged them on a plate. "I'm just getting these for Orson. I'm afraid he's going to mess up the display platter before Ruby is able to sign her first book."

Myra simply shook her head. "Oh, Orson," she said. "Sometimes I don't know what I'm going to do with that old man."

"Same as we've always done," Maggie said. "We're going to humor him, put up with him, and pamper him like the child he is." She headed back out through the swinging door into the dining room with Orson's donuts.

A short time later, a line of people stretched out into the parking lot in front of the donut shop. Maggie kept her eye on the road in front of the shop, wondering when a member of the Dogwood Mountain Police Department or the Dogwood Mountain County Sheriff's Department would show up and complain about the traffic. She had no doubt this would happen given the fact that Myra was married to the chief of police, and she was married to the county sheriff.

Ruby was seated behind the table smiling and signing autographs as people approached her. Maggie listened carefully as her best friend explained what was new about her baking cookbook. She also kept a close eye on the platter of donuts in front of Ruby, ready to run back and resupply her as needed.

"Oh, these are so divine." A short, dark haired woman beamed at Ruby. She picked up a donut and took another bite. "Can you tell me how you made these?"

"I'm sure the recipe is in the cookbook," someone from the back of the line called out.

"Oh, chill out," the woman in front of Ruby said. "I don't think it'll hurt anyone for Ruby Cobb to explain to us how she created these divine donuts."

Ruby looked at Maggie for support. Maggie shrugged her shoulders and chuckled. "Maybe speak loudly for the entire group so no one asks you the same question twice?" Her comment was met with a wave of laughter. "Meanwhile, I'll go back and get reinforcements for everyone." A ripple of applause replaced the laughter.

"Okay, I guess I can tell you how I made these black walnut and apple donuts," Ruby said. "I just started out with your basic ingredients for cake batter donuts. Enriched white flour, baking soda, salt, and so forth. Only, I added plain Greek yogurt to the batter and cinnamon. I use brown sugar instead of granulated sugar which I think lends a richer taste. Oh, and I don't cook the apples before I add them. I simply peel and chop tart apples and add them directly to the batter."

"What about the walnuts?" A woman from the back stepped out of line and held her book up for Ruby to see. Maggie emerged from the swinging door in time to see the woman shout another question at Ruby. "Does it explain in the cookbook where you sourced the black walnuts? Do you go into the history of finding the black walnuts deep in the Ozarks then breaking them apart with your own hammer and adding them to your grandmother's apple donut recipe?" The woman appeared to be about ten years older than Ruby, with spiky white-blond hair and red-rimmed glasses dominating her small face.

"Well, that's a little specific." Ruby laughed nervously. "Actually, no. I wrote this recipe myself after trying some Ozark black walnut ice cream. That's one reason why I went with the yogurt in the recipe. I wanted a creamy, richer texture. The one thing I do with the black walnuts in this recipe is toast them in the oven prior to adding them to the batter."

"Maybe that's what makes them so delicious," the woman at the head of the line said. She snagged another donut and opened her cookbook for Ruby to autograph.

"I don't think we've heard enough about where you got this recipe from, Ms. Cobb," the woman in the red rimmed glasses spoke out again. "Why don't you tell us all about where you come up with these wonderful recipes?" Maggie carefully set the new platter of donuts down on the table. She glanced sideways at Ruby then watched as the woman advanced toward the table.

"Ma'am, could you please take your place in line again?" Maggie asked. "I don't think it's fair for you to try to get ahead of the others who have been waiting just as long."

"Oh, you want to talk about fair? Why don't you ask my dead grandmother what's fair?" the woman said.

"I'm afraid I don't know what you're talking about" Maggie said. "But I'm sure Ruby will make time for you as well. Please, step back into line."

"You see, my grandmother worked her fingers to the bone on my granddaddy's Ozark farm," the woman continued. "She wrote a cookbook, too. Only, she didn't have the money for some big name publisher to pick her book up and publish it like it should have been published many years ago. Which means her family members never benefited from her unique and delicious recipes."

"I'm not sure what you're trying to say." Ruby stood up in her chair. "But I think it's time for you to leave."

"I'm sure you recognize me by now," the woman said. "Or is it my grandmother you see in my face? You do recall Laura Beth Swenson, right? After all, she's the woman you stole these recipes from!"

"I have no idea what you're talking about," Ruby said. The look on her face was sheer shock and horror. "I think it's time for you to go."

"I'm not going anywhere," the woman said. "Not until your fans hear all about how you plagiarized my grandmother's cookbook. And, not until you pay me what I am due as her granddaughter!"

Maggie glanced at Orson, who was still seated at the Old Timer's table. He held up his phone and Maggie nodded, giving him the silent order to call the police. Orson stood up and held the phone to his ear as he made his way to the far corner of the dining room.

Just then, two more women rushed in through the front doors. "Excuse us," one of them said. She stood a foot taller than the woman in the red rimmed glasses, but they shared the same face. The younger, slightly shorter woman to her right resembled her as well. "Let's go, Sarah Beth. You've caused enough trouble in here already."

"I'm not going anywhere," the woman in the red glasses snapped. She yanked her arm away from the tall woman who had made it to her side. "You're a traitor to our grandmother, you know that? You and your brat daughter, too."

"Let's go, Aunt Sarah," the younger woman said. She raised her voice higher than her mothers. "I'm not as nice as Mom. I will drag you out of here by your shirt if I have to. Let's go and leave these people alone."

"This woman stole our grandmother's recipes and you two couldn't care less," Sarah Beth shouted. She adjusted the red rimmed spectacles on her face and pointed directly at Ruby. "I challenge anyone here to look at my grandmother's cookbook and compare it to the recipes this charlatan claims she penned herself. You compare the two and tell me who was the original author."

Maggie spotted a familiar squad car in the parking

lot. Brooks Macklin unfolded himself from the driver's door and headed toward the shop.

"Great," the younger woman said. "Now you've got the police involved, Aunt Sarah."

"Hush your mouth, Heather. You have no idea what you're talking about."

CHAPTER TWO

Maggie watched as Brooks approached the women who had interrupted the book signing. The woman in the red glasses stood sandwiched between her two family members. She moved her arms and her head dramatically while she was in conversation with him.

Moments later, a second police car arrived. Another officer took over asking questions while Brooks decided to come inside the donut shop. He motioned for Maggie to join him. "As soon as Ruby takes a break, I need to talk to her in the back."

"I figured as much," Maggie said. She looked at the clock on the wall. "She has a break scheduled in about five minutes. Will that work?"

"Absolutely," Brooks said with a grin. "Is my wife in the back?"

"Your wife and an entire cooling rack filled with black walnut and apple donuts, to be precise," Maggie said. "Why don't you go on back there, and I'll send Ruby in as soon as she's ready."

"Actually, I need to talk to you as well," Brooks said. "The woman in the red glasses, who seems to be running the show, is named Sarah Beth Swenson. She claims Ruby plagiarized her grandmother's cookbook."

"She said as much," Maggie whispered. She had no desire for the remaining fans in line to hear any of her conversation. "The other woman, is that her sister?"

"Her sister, Liz, and her niece, Heather," Brooks said. "Neither of them seems to be buying into what she's claiming, however."

"I suppose this is something Ruby has gotten used to by now," Maggie said. "She's not the first author that someone has claimed stole someone else's work."

"No, but it isn't that typical for someone to come and interrupt a live book signing," Brooks said. "What worries me is how none of these women can seem to get their story straight."

"Why does that worry you?" Maggie asked. "If anything, I would think that would lend more to Ruby's credibility."

"You know I have no problem with Ruby's credibility whatsoever," Brooks reassured her. "What worries me is how upset these women are. It's one thing for someone to claim plagiarism, but another to become something of a stalker."

"I hope that's not the case here," Maggie said, shaking her head. "Ruby has been so excited to release this cookbook. She's worked on these recipes for years."

"I know, but this woman claims she has the original cookbook from her grandmother," Brooks said. "Worst case scenario, she hires an attorney and sues Ruby."

"That would be a lot better than some deranged stalker," Maggie said. She glanced at the clock again. "I think it's time for Ruby's break."

"I'll head on back then," Brooks said. He disappeared through the swinging door.

"Ladies and gentlemen," Maggie said. "I think Ruby would like a brief break. If you'd like some complimentary coffee and a donut, please feel free to approach the counter and Naomi will be glad to help you. Otherwise, Ruby will return in fifteen minutes. Thank you." Maggie stood between the line of people and Ruby, protectively walking her to the kitchen.

"What did Brooks have to say?" Ruby whispered as they walked through the swinging door.

"Hang on a second and you can find out for yourself," Maggie said. "He wants to talk to you and me both."

Brooks was standing near Myra when they entered the kitchen. He held half a black walnut and apple donut in his hand. "Are you doing okay, Ruby?" he asked.

"I'm exhausted." Ruby laughed. "But as far as the little skirmish out there goes, I'm fine."

"Have you ever seen that woman before?" Brooks asked.

"No, not in person," Ruby said. "I do think she has been writing to me, however. I've received several emails from a woman named Sarah Swenson."

"You never told me that," Maggie said. "Why didn't you say anything?"

"I don't know," Ruby said. "I get some crazy emails from time to time, but you knew that. This woman is from the other side of the state. I never thought she would show up hundreds of miles from home. Besides, her emails were never threatening or negative."

"I remember you saying something before, but not

about this person specifically," Maggie said.

"Is there any possibility there's something to her claims?" Brooks asked carefully. "I'm not at all implying I think you plagiarized the recipes, but do you have any sort of recollection of her grandmother?"

Ruby shook her head. "I've never heard of her grandmother before in my life, and to be honest with you, this is the first time I've heard that claim."

"I thought you just said she had written to you before," Brooks said.

"She has, but this is the first time she's claimed I plagiarized her grandmother's recipes. Actually, until very recently, she was always very kind. Her last couple of emails mentioned something about a few of my recipes being close to hers, but her words never seemed angry."

"So, she's claimed that you stole her recipes?" Maggie said. "And just now she's claiming they were actually her grandmother's recipes?"

"That basically sums it up," Ruby said. She turned to Brooks. "Do you think we ought to shut the book signing down?"

"No, not at all," Brooks said. "I'm waiting for my backup to come and tell me that he got the contact information from Sarah Beth and her sister and niece.

After that, we'll either bring Sarah Beth in for more questioning or we'll let her go with a warning. I don't see any danger in you continuing your book signing."

"I think we ought to just move forward with the rest of the day," Ruby said.

"Please let me know if you hear anything else from this woman," Brooks said.

"You don't think there's any reason to cancel any of her upcoming book signings, do you?" Maggie asked. For once, she wished Ruby's new book agent was on hand to take care of these matters.

Brooks shook his head. "I don't think that's necessary, but I would let your people know what's going on. Maybe giving them a heads-up now can stop any further interruptions."

"I was wondering where your editor and agent are," Myra interrupted. "Why aren't either of them here?"

Ruby shrugged. "Since this is my home turf, neither of them saw any reason to drive up here from Little Rock," she explained.

"Fair enough," Brooks answered for his wife. "Still, I think my next phone call would be to them."

"That's my plan," Ruby said. "But for now, I think I will head back out and sign a few more books."

CHAPTER THREE

Maggie quickly forgot about the drama from earlier in the day. She was eager to rush home after work. Brett had promised her a home cooked meal, and Maggie was not one to shy away from her husband's cooking.

She was also eager to share with him the news of the day. Ruby Cobb was not just her best friend and business partner, she was also one of her husband's closest friends. Over the years, her small family had grown to include friends. Several years back, when Maggie first returned home to Dogwood Mountain, she came without a friend or anyone in her life. Before that, her son Bradley was away in the Navy and her ex-husband had dominated their relationship.

In the past several years, Maggie had not only fallen in love with the man of her dreams, but she had found a family and a group of friends that couldn't have been closer had they shared the same biology. Her adult son even referred to her best friend as his Aunt Ruby. His little boy, Wyatt, had done the same since he began talking.

Even though she'd been trying to ignore it, there was something about the situation earlier that had rattled Maggie. Perhaps it was this protective nature she had found since becoming part of this greater family, but she felt the sudden need to circle the wagons around her best friend. Why Sarah Beth was at the book signing, she was not sure. The fact that the woman's sister and niece had been there as well disturbed her, too.

"What's on your mind, babe?" Brett asked. He was standing outside the back door of their house with a large metal spatula in one hand and a meat thermometer in the other. Luckily for Maggie, Brett's idea of home cooking involved thick T-bone steaks, mashed potatoes, and grilled corn on the cob. Her mouth watered the second she caught a whiff of the meat sizzling on the grill.

"I'm surprised you didn't hear about what happened today from Brooks," she said, getting out of her car.

"He left me a message earlier, but we didn't have

time to get into things too much," Brett said. "It was on my personal cell phone, by the way. I would have been more concerned if it been something official from work."

"You don't have to justify the way you do your job to me," Maggie said. She placed one arm around him and leaned in to smell the steaks. "That is heaven on a grill."

"I sure hope you think so when you sit down for dinner," Brett said. "Anyway, what happened today?"

"Ruby held a book signing for her new cookbook at the donut shop, and she debuted a brand new donut variety. Something that is included in the cookbook."

"A new donut variety? I trust you brought home samples for your husband to try," Brett said.

"Of course. How can you ask me such a question? Anyway, during the book signing, this disturbed woman jumped out of line and started accusing Ruby of plagiarizing her grandmother's cookbook."

"Wow. Is that what Brooks wants to talk to me about?" he asked. "I guess it got pretty serious if Brooks was involved."

"Yeah, it got a little serious," Maggie said. "The weird part was that the woman's niece and sister were there. They tried to pull her away and calm her down."

"Why is that weird?" Brett asked. "Maybe they came along for the trip and didn't know what she was planning to pull in front of everyone."

"I don't know. Maybe I'm just overthinking this, but it turns out, this is a woman Ruby has heard from before. Although, the claims about her grandmother are new, and she is from the other side of the state."

"I imagine that people drive from all over to attend book signings," Brett said. "I'm not sure that makes this any stranger one way or the other. I bet she never shared with her sister and her niece what her intentions were once she got here. They probably just thought they were going to a book signing with her."

"You're probably right," Maggie said. "It's just that there's something about this situation that has me feeling a little uneasy."

"Of course, I'm right," Brett said with a grin. "Hang out here for a sec. I forgot something in the kitchen, and I think I better grab my phone while I'm in there." Brett handed his large grill tongs over to Maggie with the order not to turn the steaks quite yet. He rushed inside and reappeared a moment later with a jar of seasoning and his cell phone. He scrolled the phone screen as he walked.

"Honey, is everything okay?" Maggie asked. She

waited for him to approach the grill before handing the tongs back off to him.

"I don't know for sure," Brett said, not taking his eyes off the screen. "Hold on a minute. I think I need to call in." He handed the tongs back to her for a second time.

Maggie turned her attention to the sizzling meat on the grill as Brett walked toward the detached garage with his phone up to his ear. He planted one hand on his hip and stopped, leaning over, and staring hard at the gravel below. Maggie felt her heart quicken a little. She knew his body language well enough to know that something was going on at work.

"Oh, honey," Maggie whispered to herself. "Not an interruption. Not tonight."

Brett turned away from the garage and headed back, stuffing his phone into his pocket as he walked. He shook his head and glanced at the steaks on the grill. "I am so sorry," he began. He leaned over and kissed her on the forehead. "I have to go."

"What's going on?" Maggie asked. "Can you tell me?"

Brett shook his head again. "All I can tell you is that someone discovered the body of a woman just outside of the city limits. I have no more information than that."

"Which means that you have to go because that is your jurisdiction," Maggie said with an exaggerated sigh.

"Yes, I'm sorry," Brett said. This time he kissed her on the lips. "Just take those off in about five minutes and I'll eat mine when I get home."

"That's what I get for marrying a law man," Maggie said with a sad smile.

After Brett left the driveway, Maggie texted Ruby. "Hey, Brett had to go into work. Do you want to share a steak with me?"

The reply came a few minutes later after Maggie had already removed the steaks from the grill. "So sorry," Ruby wrote. "Something came up. I can't. Talk to you at work."

"Well, I guess everyone is abandoning me tonight," Maggie said as she set the steaks aside to cool. She decided to save her appetite for later when Brett returned home.

By the time Brett walked back through the door, it was just past midnight. Maggie had fallen asleep on the couch with her legs curled up under a blanket. She woke when Brett sat down next to her. "Maggie, I need to talk to you," he said quietly.

"Can we talk in the morning?" Maggie patted his

arm with her hand and repositioned herself on the couch. "Let's just go to bed."

"No. I need you to get up for a moment," Brett said. He pulled the blanket off her and stood up.

"Let's go to bed. It's late," Maggie said, still half asleep.

"I need you to listen to me," Brett said sternly. "Get up."

"What's going on?" Maggie asked, suddenly waking up. She sat up on the edge of the couch and looked at him.

"The body we found was of a woman in her mid-sixties," Brett began. "According to her identification, her name is Sarah Beth Swenson."

"Oh my gosh," Maggie gasped. "That's the woman with the red glasses from earlier today. She's the one that caused a big stink at Ruby's book signing."

"I am quite aware of that fact," Brett said. "We have a little bit of a problem."

"What is the problem?" Maggie asked. She didn't want to know the answer. Part of her knew it wasn't going to be good.

"The problem is that the woman was strangled to death. We have a dead woman in her own car with ligature marks around her neck," Brett explained. "She had two books in her car with her when she died. One of them was a handwritten journal containing recipes, and the other was Ruby's latest cookbook."

"Oh, no," Maggie said. "Please tell me you know who did it already."

"I don't know much yet, but her family seems fairly convinced that they know who did it."

"Please don't say it," Maggie said. "Better yet, please just don't let it be true."

Brett nodded and turned his back to her. He paced around the living room for a moment. "They're pointing the finger at Ruby, but the real problem is, Ruby can't account for her whereabouts tonight."

"She can't account for her whereabouts? I texted her and she replied to me," Maggie said. "It was right after you left. I invited her over for dinner, but she said she couldn't come over."

Brett shook his head and turned back to her. "That isn't good news," he said. "I really, really wish she would have come over here for dinner tonight."

CHAPTER FOUR

Maggie paced the kitchen floor for over an hour while Brett urged her to come to bed and get some sleep. No matter how hard she tried to lie in bed and force herself to go to sleep, her mind raced with thoughts about her best friend. Was Ruby about to be charged with murder?

Brett didn't indicate that she was on the short list for an arrest, but the fact that she couldn't account for her whereabouts left Maggie feeling hollow inside. She wanted to force time to move forward faster so she could get to work in the morning and ask her friend in person where she had been.

Morning finally came after a sleepless night. She stumbled into the kitchen of the donut shop and began mechanically going through the day's chores. She watched the clock and began to wonder when Ruby would arrive. Around half past six, Maggie tried Ruby's phone for the third time. She gave up and placed a call to Brett.

"I can't get ahold of Ruby," Maggie said as soon as he answered. "Please, please tell me she hasn't been arrested."

"She hasn't. Not to my knowledge, anyway," Brett said. "It is concerning that you can't get ahold of her, though. Do you want me to run by her house?"

"As long as you won't end up arresting her," Maggie said, only halfway kidding.

"I have no plans to arrest Ruby," Brett said defensively. "It's still so early in the investigation. There's no reason to even think that way."

"Okay, but last night you said you wished she had come to our house for dinner," Maggie said. "I thought you said that because it would have given her an alibi."

"Maybe, but just because this woman came in and interrupted the book signing, it doesn't mean there's a reason to suspect Ruby of murder."

"It doesn't? That's good to hear," Maggie said. "I guess I just assumed she would be the first in line after what they found."

"If there had been a physical altercation, or Ruby

had engaged in a shouting match with her, we might be looking at that," Brett said. "But so far, it's just not enough that her cookbook was there."

"You don't think Ruby had anything to do with this woman's death, do you?"

Brett hesitated before he answered. "No, of course not, but I do get the feeling that there's something going on with her. I just can't put my finger on it yet."

"I'm not really sure what you mean," Maggie said. "You think there's something going on with her?"

"How often have you known Ruby not to be able to account for her whereabouts?" Brett asked.

"Not ever," Maggie said. "She did act a little strange last night."

"It just seems like she's been a bit off lately," Brett said. "Of course, that's not my official statement as a police officer or anything."

"I like it when you distinguish between yourself as my husband and as the county sheriff," Maggie said.

Maggie continued to work through the morning routine. She was glad when Naomi and Myra showed up to help out. She did her best to deflect questions, but in the end, she had to explain what was going on.

"Have you heard from Brett yet?" Myra asked her just after the doors opened to the public.

"Nothing yet," Maggie said. She smiled and tried to play off her concern, but she was beginning to worry.

"Where is Ruby at this morning?" Orson asked when he came in for his morning cup of coffee.

"She's taking the morning," Maggie said. The dining room was full of waiting customers. She returned to the counter and retrieved a full pot of coffee and then made her way back to the Old Timer's table. She leaned in and whispered in his ear. "Come back and see me in the kitchen after a while. I don't want to explain everything right now."

Five minutes later, Orson burst through the swinging door. "You can't do that to me, you know," he grumbled.

"Do what to you?" Maggie asked. She handed him a cinnamon roll and pointed to the wooden stool in front of the baker's table.

"You can't drop a bombshell that something is going on and then expect me to wait until you have a chance to explain it," Orson said. "Is Ruby alright? Is everything okay?"

Maggie let out a long sigh and pulled a stool in front of his. She took a seat and patted his knee. "I'm not sure if Ruby is okay or not," she began. "You might as well hear it from me first. Do you remember the woman who raised such a fuss yesterday during the book signing?"

"Yeah, how could I forget?"

"Brett got a call last night and had to go into work," Maggie explained. "When he got home around midnight, he told me that the woman, Sarah Beth Swenson, had been found murdered in her car on the highway."

Orson gasped. "Oh, you're kidding." He set the cinnamon roll down and placed his hands over hers. "They've arrested Ruby, haven't they? That's what's going on, right?"

Maggie shook her head. "No, she hasn't been arrested, but according to Brett, she can't account for her whereabouts last night, and she didn't come into work today. She was a no call, no show. Brett is going by her house to check on her. We're all kind of sitting around waiting to hear from him."

"So, you haven't heard from Ruby all morning?" Orson asked. Maggie shook her head and squeezed his hands together with hers.

"I think all we can do is stay as busy as possible while we wait to hear from Brett," Maggie said. She patted Orson's hands and stood up. "Which means I need to get busy with the preparations for the boxed lunches. It's funny, I get so used to Ruby being here and doing all of these little things herself. It's so empty around here without her around."

Orson walked back out to the Old Timer's table. Maggie caught glimpses of him through the swinging door and hoped that she had done the right thing by telling him the truth. Since his stroke a while back, she was always watching him for signs of distress. The last thing she needed was for something bad to happen to Orson.

Around noon, Orson made his way back to the kitchen once again. "Have you heard anything?" he asked. "Anything at all?"

"No, nothing at all," Maggie said. They were in the middle of the lunch rush. She moved quickly to assemble more boxed lunches for waiting customers.

"Well, I just came back here to let you all know I'm going," Orson said.

Maggie stopped what she was doing and looked at him. "You're going? You always stay here for most of the day. Are you feeling okay, Orson?" she asked. "I can have Myra drive you home."

"No, I'm not going home," Orson said. "I'm driving out to the farm. I want to go check on Ruby myself. I'm sick and tired of waiting around here for your husband to get back with us."

"Are you sure that's a good idea?" Maggie asked. "You look a little tired to me."

"Maggie, stop it," Orson snapped. "You're worried about your best friend. You worry every day about your husband. I know you worry about me, but stop adding me to your list of things to be extra worried about. I am fine. I'm going to get in my car and go for a drive. It's something I do every day. Now, if you'll excuse me, I have a friend to go check on."

"I'm sorry, Orson," Maggie said. "I'm not trying to micromanage you."

"Good. Then don't," he said. "Keep your phone on. I'll text you as soon as I get there," he called back to her over his shoulder.

Maggie did her best to go back to work and focus on the job at hand. She waited until close to one o'clock before she gave up and called Brett.

"Anything?" Myra asked when she returned to the kitchen.

"It went straight to his voicemail," Maggie said, shoving her phone back in her back pocket.

"What about Orson?" Myra asked.

"I haven't heard a thing yet," Maggie said. "I'm

not sure that I want to call him before he reaches out to me. He's a bit sensitive these days."

"Yeah, well, I think he can take my phone call," Myra said. She dismissed herself to the office and pressed her phone to her ear.

"What's that all about?" Naomi asked when she ventured into the kitchen from the dining room.

"Myra is going to get in touch with Orson to see what is going on with Ruby," Maggie said.

"Because you're too chicken to call him?" Naomi asked.

"He told me to let him handle things," Maggie said. "The guy is basically our dad, you know. Who wants to go against that?"

"True," Naomi said.

"Did you talk to him?" Maggie asked Myra when she returned a moment later.

Myra nodded. "I think it's a waste of time for me to try to explain," she said. "You need to get over there right now. We'll cover you. Just go as soon as possible."

CHAPTER FIVE

Maggie wasted no time. She left Myra and Naomi in charge of the donut shop and headed straight for Ruby's farm. She was surprised to see Brett's pickup truck in the driveway. Orson's old car was parked behind him. She headed straight for the front door and knocked, but there was no answer.

Maggie wandered around to the kitchen door in the back of the house, the door she was used to using. She knocked a few times and waited, but there was still no response. She slowly turned the handle and realized that the door was open.

"Hello? Ruby? Is anyone home?" Maggie called into the empty kitchen.

"Down here," Brett's voice called. Maggie headed for the basement door and pulled it open.

"Are you all down there?" she asked. She hesitated at the top of the stairs.

"Yeah, we're down here," Orson's voice called out. Maggie descended the steps to the basement quickly. She'd only been in the basement of the farmhouse a handful of times. Everything looked as it always had. On one side, Ruby had installed shelves for the garden produce she canned every year. Two freezers lined the wall next to the shelves.

On the other side, Ruby had enclosed the small finished-in area. It was set up to look like an office, although it was more of an archive then a functioning office. Copies of Ruby's multiple cookbooks lined bookshelves. There were binders of loose papers and stacks of spiral notebooks where the former executive chef kept her notes from various cooking experiences. She once explained to Maggie how she would fill up notebook after notebook when she was working on a new cookbook.

At first, Maggie spotted Brett and Orson alone. She looked around for any sign of her best friend. "What is going on around here?" she asked. "Where's Ruby?"

"Over here," Ruby's voice, hoarse and thin, called out from somewhere in the corner. Maggie walked around the large oak desk at the far end of the room and found her seated on the floor. Two empty wine bottles were at her feet.

"Ruby?" Maggie walked behind the desk and lowered herself slowly to the floor next to her best friend. "Are you okay?"

Ruby shook her head. "No, I'm not okay," she said. "I'm afraid I've hit a wall."

"It seems as if Ruby has been down here since the problem occurred at her book signing yesterday," Brett said. He nodded to the wine bottles on the floor.

Maggie reached for her friend's hand. "What's wrong?"

Ruby merely shrugged and smiled sadly. "I don't honestly know. I think maybe I'm having some sort of a breakdown."

"Why don't you start by telling me what happened when you left the donut shop yesterday?" Maggie noticed a dozen or so binders open on the floor on the other side of the desk. It looked as if someone had pulled them off the shelves and let them fall where they landed.

"I don't know," Ruby said. "I decided after a little while to come down here and double check some of the recipes I had gathered for the newest cookbook. I guess that's when everything got turned around for me."

"What do you mean?" Maggie asked. She did her best to keep her voice gentle. "How did you get turned around?"

There was another shrug from Ruby. "I just started double checking my sources on some of those recipes," she said. "You know, just to reassure myself that what that woman said wasn't true."

"And what did you find out?" Maggie said. "I mean, I already know the answer. You realized that your sources were legitimate and that you hadn't committed plagiarism of any kind, right?"

"Not exactly," Ruby said. "I'm more confused than ever."

"It looks like you hit the bottle pretty hard, too," Orson mumbled. "I'm sure that didn't help your confusion."

"Orson," Maggie warned.

"No, he's right," Ruby said. "I started drinking one glass of wine. Pretty soon it turned into one bottle, then another. I remember that you texted me at some point last night."

"Ruby," Maggie said, glancing up at Brett. "I'm sure you've heard by now what happened. Do you have any memory whatsoever of leaving here? Did you go anywhere?"

"Please don't tell me you're questioning whether she killed that woman or not," Orson interjected.

"Of course she isn't," Ruby said. "I know what you're asking, and I did not go anywhere. I was here the entire time. You're worried they might come after me as a suspect." This time, Ruby was the one that shot a look in Brett's direction.

"I've already checked the footage from her doorbell camera outside," Brett said. "Her alibi is as tight as it can be. She didn't go anywhere."

"Ruby, I didn't mean to imply that you might have been the one to harm that woman," Maggie said.

"I know," Ruby looked up at her and smiled. "You're worried about me. I get that. A murder was committed and it's rather odd timing, given what happened at my book signing yesterday. I was caught up in my feelings last night, but I didn't go anywhere. There's no danger of being accused of it."

Maggie let out a sigh of relief. "I am so glad to hear that," she said. "I never doubted you for a minute, but not everyone is your best friend."

"She's right there," Brett said. He held up his cell phone. "I'm getting about three messages every hour from the family of the deceased woman. They are upset and wondering what I'm doing about the investigation."

"What are you still doing here, then?" Ruby asked. "You don't need to be here babysitting me anymore. I'm fine. I had a huge fit of self-doubt and imposter syndrome last night. I had to prove to myself that I wasn't the fraud I was accused of being. I guess I went a little too far with the wine."

"You guess you went too far with the wine?" Orson said, raising his eyebrows.

Ruby chuckled. "I absolutely went too far with the wine," Ruby said. "You aren't wrong, but I didn't go anywhere. My truck is parked in the same place it was when I got home from work yesterday."

"Part of the reason I'm here is because of the investigation," Brett said. "I wanted to make sure I was armed with the correct information before I went back and faced the woman's family."

"Why? Are they saying something about me?" Ruby asked.

"Let's just say your name has been thrown around a little bit," Brett said.

"What do you mean by that?" Maggie asked.

"He means that the family of the dead woman has already started throwing around accusations that it was Ruby who did the deed," Orson said.

Brett nodded. "More or less, but I'm satisfied after looking at your camera footage that there's no way you were involved. Not that I didn't know before, but I had to be sure I could prove that to other people."

"Of course," Ruby said. "I understand. You have to do what you have to do for your job." She began to slowly stand up. She rubbed the small of her back and twisted her head around trying to relieve the pressure in her neck.

"Are you a little sore?" Orson asked with a grin. "I don't recommend spending the night on the floor."

"You can say that again," Ruby said.

"I have to get going," Brett announced. "Ruby, are you good?"

"I'm good," she said. "If not, I have a feeling these two aren't going to give me any peace until I am."

Brett made his way over to Maggie and kissed her on the cheek before he headed back up the stairs.

"I guess I better get back home, too," Orson said. "You never know when they're going to need me."

"Do you mean Lexi?" Maggie asked, referring to Brooks and Myra's daughter.

Orson shook his head. "No, I'm talking about Brooks and Myra. Those two need me far more than Lexi ever has." Orson leaned over and pecked Ruby on the forehead, something Maggie had never seen him do before. He slowly went up the stairs. She heard him walk across the kitchen floor and out the back door.

"I suppose we should head upstairs ourselves," Ruby said.

"That sounds like a good idea," Maggie agreed.

"Can I get you something to drink?" Ruby asked when they reached the top of the stairs.

"Sure," Maggie said. "I would love some of your sweet tea, with a side of the truth about what the heck is going on with you."

CHAPTER SIX

Ruby stared into the refrigerator for a long moment. She pulled out the pitcher of tea and set it on the counter below the cabinet where she stored her glasses. Maggie waited patiently for her to answer the question she had just posed.

"I told you," Ruby said at last. "I just had a moment. I came home and started tearing through my notebooks to prove to myself where my recipes came from."

"Did you honestly have any doubt?" Maggie asked.

"Yes, no. I don't know," Ruby said. She filled two glass tumblers with ice and poured the tea over the top.

"Ruby, I have never known you to fall victim to

so much self-doubt," Maggie said. "It's almost like you believed that woman."

"I've been writing cookbooks for nearly twenty years," she explained. "I have spent hours and hours researching, interviewing people, finding new recipes anywhere and everywhere I could. You may not know this, but before you came back to Dogwood Mountain, I spent a lot of time wandering around the Ozark hills talking to some old timers. I copied recipes down before they could be lost by time."

"Did you ever meet Miss Swenson's grandmother?"

"That's what I came home to figure out," Ruby said. "When I use a recipe, I've always been very careful to give credit where it is due. I have never once stolen a recipe from a single living soul, but I tore apart my office looking for any reference to the Swenson family."

"You didn't find any, did you?" Maggie asked.

Ruby shook her head. "No, but that didn't help my imposter syndrome."

"What is imposter syndrome?" Maggie said. "You've mentioned it twice now."

"Imposter syndrome is the curse of anyone who puts themselves out there for public scrutiny," Ruby explained. "It affects writers, creative people, artists of all kinds, even cookbook authors. Basically, it's your brain telling you that you're not anything but a fraud or a fake."

"How long have you been dealing with this?" Maggie asked.

"Since my first book was published," Ruby said.

"Is that why you wouldn't come over to my house for dinner last night?"

Ruby laughed. "No, I didn't come over because I was sitting on my rear end on my office floor."

"Fair enough," Maggie said. She took a long sip of her tea and sat down at the kitchen table. "Ruby, do you have proof that the recipes you got for the new cookbook were not from that lady's grandmother? Did you find any reference to the Swenson family at all?"

"Absolutely none," Ruby said. "Why are you asking? Do you think we're going to have more issues?"

"I think a woman has died, and I don't like the connection she has to you," Maggie said. "I know her family is grieving, and grief sometimes causes people to say and do things that aren't quite right. I guess I just want to be prepared in case they decide to push the matter a little bit more."

"I don't mean to sound insensitive, but they can

push all they want to," Ruby said. "I'm sorry they lost their loved one, but I had nothing to do with it. And I never had anything to do with anyone by the name of Swenson."

An hour later, Maggie headed back home. She checked in with Myra and Naomi at the donut shop and decided there was no need for her to go back into work. Before she left, Ruby promised to be at work bright and early the following morning.

As she pulled into the driveway, her cell phone chimed. "Don't wait up for me," Brett texted. "It's going to be a late night."

Maggie texted him back quickly. She had no doubt that the murder investigation would keep him later than usual. In the short time they had been married, she had come to understand that any large investigation often meant late working hours.

"I figured as much," Maggie wrote back. "See you later." She hated to see him so busy, but with a murder on his hands, it couldn't be helped.

After she changed out of her work clothes, Maggie headed into the kitchen. She opened the freezer and searched around for a moment, then selected a small package of chicken breasts from the refrigerator and set them in the sink until she was ready to make dinner. She had some time on her hands and decided to whip up something special. Brett would be surprised to receive a hot meal from home while he was still at the office.

Not long after, Maggie loaded the hot chicken roll ups and twice-baked potatoes into her car. She drove out of town toward the sheriff's department. She wanted her visit to be a surprise for Brett, but texted his secretary to let her know she was going to stop by.

The office staff welcomed her with open arms anytime she came in, and today was no exception. Maggie carried the insulated food bag through the door Brett's secretary opened for her. After the events of the past few days, she enjoyed the positive feeling that came from doing something nice for someone else.

"He's down the hall in the conference room," Maryellen told her. "You can leave his dinner in the office, and I'll pop my head in to let him know you're here."

"That's okay," Maggie said. "I'll walk down there and wait for him. I'm sure you're eager to get home."

Maryellen smiled. "I am," she admitted. "If you just wait outside the conference room, he'll see you and step out. Just don't knock or open the door yourself. You know the drill."

"I know," Maggie said. She opened the office

door and set the food bag on the table against the wall. The food was still piping hot and would remain that way for some time. She pulled the door closed behind her and walked down the hallway to the pair of conference rooms at the end. She made sure to walk past the window on the doorway so Brett would see her, then took a seat in the small waiting area to pass the time until he emerged.

As soon as she took a seat, she heard a slight ruckus in the conference room. She could hear the sound of chairs scraping across the floor and raised voices. The door flew open, and Brett stepped out. His face was flushed red and glowing with sweat. Heather and Liz, Sarah Beth Swenson's niece and sister, stood right behind him.

"Now I see what's going on around here," Heather shouted. She pointed her finger at Maggie. "This is who you're married to? The owner of the donut shop?"

"What difference does that make?" Maggie asked. She stood up from her chair. "Why does my marriage have anything to do with you?"

"Because it's clear you two are deliberately stalling the investigation into my sister's murder," Liz said. "I find this very suspicious."

"I can assure you that my wife has nothing to do

with my work as the sheriff," Brett said. "She also had nothing to do with anyone's death."

"So, because she's your wife, you automatically rule her out as a suspect?" Liz snapped.

"A suspect? Why would you think I had anything to do with your sister's death?" Maggie asked. "I only met her for a few minutes!"

"You might have wanted her dead after the claims she made against your employee," Heather said.

Maggie closed her eyes for a moment, trying to steel herself against the ridiculousness of their words. "I never knew your sister existed until the signing," she said. "I didn't seek her out. She came to my donut shop. I don't have a clue what she drives or where she might have been."

"We've all been staying at the Dogwood House," Heather said. "My aunt was so eager to come here. She loves Ruby's work, and we thought it would be a nice trip for all of us. Only, I just found out that you once owned the same house we're staying in. How convenient is that?"

Maggie shook her head. "I never owned the Dogwood House," she said. "My great-aunt did. I spent my childhood there, but never once owned it."

"What difference does it make, anyway?" Brett

asked. "Whether she owned the house or not bears absolutely nothing on this case."

"It means that this entire town is related to you," Liz sneered. "And my sister is dead. Your husband wouldn't lift a finger to investigate you if you were the top suspect."

"For the record, my wife was with me at home when the murder occurred," Brett said. "That's not debatable. That is an indisputable fact."

"Fine, but that doesn't clear her employee," Liz said.

"Full disclosure, Ruby Cobb is more than my employee. She is my business partner and my closest friend," Maggie said. "If she was a suspect in your sister's death, my husband would investigate her to the fullest. Or he would hand the investigation over to someone else who is not personally involved."

"And we're supposed to believe that?" Heather rolled her eyes.

"She is exactly right," Brett said.

"Then why don't we ask the police in the town to investigate her death and not you?" Heather said. "Why do we need the sheriff?"

"Because her body was found beyond city limits," Brett said. "That falls outside of the Dogwood Mountain Police Department's jurisdiction."

"Okay, so ask the chief of police to take over anyway," Heather suggested. "If you're so set on being transparent and all."

Maggie chuckled. She walked in a circle and shook her head.

"Is there something funny about that?" Heather snapped at her.

"Not funny, but ironic," Maggie said. "Brooks Macklin is the police chief, and he is married to one of our employees."

"Are you serious?" Heather asked. Her eyes widened. "I swear I need to call in the state police just to get things done properly around here."

"Call them," Brett said. "I'll get you the number. Have them come in and go over every square inch of my investigation. I guarantee you they will be here less than two hours before they realize there is no possible way my wife or Ruby Cobb had opportunity or motive to murder your aunt."

"Okay, I would like that number, then," Heather said. "Let them come in and take over here. At least we will know there is something being done."

"Fine," Brett said. "Hang on a minute and I will be right back." He turned and headed down the hallway to his office.

"Mom, we ought to just go," Heather said

suddenly. "I don't think we need to call in the state police. This has gone too far. We should just let the sheriff do his job."

Liz stared at her daughter for a moment. "Are you feeling alright?" she asked. "You are the one who is pushing this so hard. Why are you backing off now?"

Maggie remained quiet in the background, hopeful they would say more, but Brett returned too fast for them to say anything else. "Here," he said, handing over a sticky note with a number scrawled across it.

Liz reached for it and snatched it away. "Now maybe we can get some answers, and a real investigation going."

CHAPTER SEVEN

"I'm so sorry," Maggie said. She fussed with the food carrier while Brett took a seat behind his desk. "I just wanted to bring something hot for you to eat for dinner."

"You have nothing to apologize for," he told her. "And you have no idea how much I appreciate dinner."

"Okay, but I interrupted your interview, and my presence apparently stirred something up in those two."

"The interview wasn't going anywhere even before you showed up," Brett said. "I don't know what to make of those two."

"What do you mean?" Maggie asked.

Brett shook his head and accepted a plate of food

from her. "This smells so good," he said, then sighed. "These women come in here demanding to know what we're doing about their relative's murder. I filled them in on what has been going on, but that isn't good enough for them."

"I hate to say it, but that doesn't sound too unusual. You've certainly dealt with demanding questions before," Maggie pointed out.

"Yeah, but the second I start to dig in a little deeper and ask them questions that might help with the investigation, they both shut down," he said. "They keep insisting that this all has to do with their grandmother and Ruby stealing her recipes."

"But they won't answer the rest of your questions?"

"Nope," Brett said. "The truth of the matter is, they behaved like they wanted to block me at every turn. They seem to have already made up their minds about what happened to Sarah Beth."

After they ate, Maggie left the rest of the food at the office with him. He promised to be home as soon as he could, but the possibility of state police swooping down on him over the investigation meant more hours and time in the office, making sure everything was in order and simple for them to understand.

Back home, Maggie picked her phone up and

browsed through her messages, looking for anything more from Ruby. It disturbed her that her best friend was taking the accusations of a stranger so hard. It disturbed her even more that the family members of a dead woman insisted that Ruby was somehow responsible for the death. They had even suggested Maggie herself might be the killer. Why were they so quick to assume the murder had anything to do with either of them?

Maggie decided to call Ruby and check in on her. She had a feeling that she might be feeling down again. The phone rang and went to voicemail before she picked up. Maggie decided not to leave a message but sent her a text instead.

"I wanted to check in on you and make sure that you're doing alright," Maggie wrote.

Ruby called a moment later. "I'm sorry," she said as soon as Maggie picked up the phone. "I was downstairs looking through things again."

"Why?" Maggie asked. "Did something happen?"

"I was still searching for any mention of Laura Beth Swenson," Ruby admitted.

"But why?" Maggie asked. "Surely you're not convinced that you might have accidentally committed plagiarism?"

"I don't know what I am," Ruby said. "I've never

doubted myself so much. Even when I said before that I was sure I wasn't responsible, I'm not sure how much I actually believe that."

"Why does this bother you so much? You've already searched thorough your things, and you don't remember this family at all. I hate that you're second guessing yourself like this."

"I wish I knew," Ruby admitted. "I can't seem to shake the feeling. I've pored over every single note I've taken since the last time I interviewed some of the old timers in the hills."

"And still found no reference to their grandmother," Maggie reminded her.

"Not one, but this is still really bothering me. I haven't felt like this for a very long time."

Maggie ended her phone call with Ruby, not convinced that she had done any good by reaching out. She ended up being even more concerned about her friend than she had been before. She wasn't sure how much of Ruby's current state of mind had to do with Sarah Beth Swenson's accusations or the mystery surrounding her death.

Her thoughts turned back to the woman's death. She didn't know much about what had happened, aside from the information Brett had passed along. Sarah Beth had been found dead in her car with marks around her neck. No weapon had been recovered. No motive had been discovered. Aside from the hand-written recipe book she had with her, the only other evidence was a copy of Ruby's latest cookbook.

As far as she knew, no one had suggested any other theories. It was possible that the assailant was someone the woman knew, but it was just as possible that the killer was a random stranger. Her car was found out on the highway, accessible to innumerable amounts of people passing up and down the road.

Without much evidence to go on, it was possible that Sarah Beth's murder might not be solved for a very long time. There were endless possibilities of possible suspects. She had no doubt that the presence of the state police would do nothing to help narrow down the list of suspects.

Aside from the fact that Sarah Beth had claimed Ruby had stolen her grandmother's recipes, Maggie knew very little about her, or the other members of her family. Her family was from the far southeastern corner of the state. Her grandmother had passed away and left a handful of recipes she claimed Ruby had somehow stolen from her and used in her cookbook.

Ruby indicated that she had been hearing from the woman for some time, though the claims about her grandmother's recipes had surfaced only at the book signing. Maggie ventured into her small office at home and took a seat in front of her laptop. She opened the lid and sat in front of the screen for several moments, not sure what she was doing there.

"Let's start with Grandma," she muttered to herself and opened her internet browser. She typed in the name of the woman, Laura Beth Swenson, to look up her obituary. She focused her search in the southeastern region of the state. When the search turned up nothing, she widened her search to the rest of the state.

Nothing came up still, so she expanded the search to the neighboring states including Arkansas and Tennessee. When she found no obituaries, Maggie began to wonder if she had the right name. She returned to the main search engine page and searched again, this time for the woman's name alone and not for her obituary. Instantly she found a woman named Laura Beth Swenson residing in a nursing home in Poplar Bluff, Missouri.

Maggie sat back in her desk chair and stared at the screen. She opened another tab and entered the name into a people search website. The search returned Laura Beth's name along with a list of her relatives and close associates including Heather Swenson and her mother, Liz.

"Laura Beth Swenson is still alive?" Maggie stared at the screen. She reread the screen over and over. Sarah Beth had claimed that Ruby stole her dead grandmother's recipes, right? She closed her eyes and forced herself to remember the interaction. She was starting to doubt her own memory.

Unless there was some mistake, Sarah Beth was either confused or a liar. On top of that, her sister and her niece had to have been in on the lie as well.

CHAPTER EIGHT

"It's so good to see you back here today," Myra said to Ruby the following morning. Ruby smiled, but Maggie could tell by the shadows under her eyes that she was still not getting much sleep.

"Have you heard anything from those two women since the other day?" Naomi asked. It was just an hour after opening, and already the donut shop lobby was full of waiting customers.

Ruby shook her head. "I haven't heard anything, thank goodness," she said.

"Nothing they have to say is worth listening to anyway," Orson grumbled. He was standing a few feet away from Ruby at the prep table. He had spent more time in the kitchen over the past week then he had since his retirement from working at the donut shop.

"They did lose a loved one, Orson," Ruby said.

"That doesn't give them the right to go around claiming people are responsible," Orson replied. "Especially when they don't know what they're talking about."

"I think it's reasonable they're upset," Ruby said. Her shoulders were hunched forward as she shredded fresh apples for her famous apple slaw.

"Of course it's reasonable," Maggie weighed in. "However, it's not fair they look for blame where there is none to be found."

"Have you heard anything from Brett about the investigation?" Myra asked her then. "Brooks won't say a word one way or another."

"Honestly, I got a little bit of a first-hand view of how the investigation is going last night," Maggie said.

"How's that?" Orson asked.

"I decided to take a hot meal over to Brett's office last night," Maggie explained. "When I got there, his secretary, Maryellen, told me to wait outside the conference room where he was conducting an interview. I guess the interview subjects must have seen me pass by the window and that started a whole thing. He was interviewing Heather and Liz. As soon as they saw me, they came out swinging with new accusations."

"Accusations about what?" Orson asked.

"About Brett and his conduct during the investigation of Sarah Beth's murder," Maggie said. "They even managed to throw in an accusation against me as the potential killer."

The last comment caused Ruby to drop what she was doing and turn around and face her. "You mean to tell me those two actually accused you?" she asked. "Please tell me I'm misunderstanding you."

"You're not," Maggie said. "They came right out and accused me of it, and then they accused Brett of being irresponsible with his investigation. One of them started to insist that they call in the state police to take over."

"Oh, I bet they'll be happy to hear from them." Myra chuckled. "They just love it when people call them in when they have a bone to pick with the local sheriff."

"I bet Brett was pretty upset about it," Ruby said.

"Not one bit," Maggie said. "As a matter of fact, he welcomed it."

"Does that mean they'll be taking over?" Naomi asked.

"It's hard to say," Maggie said. "Because just as soon as they got the number, the younger one, Heather, backed way off. I don't know why, but she started rethinking her position, I guess."

"That's strange," Myra said.

"Tell me about it," Maggie said, heading back out into the dining room. "I wouldn't have believed it myself." She faced a long line in front of the register when she walked through the swinging door. Immediately, she went to work and waited on her customers.

An hour later, she returned to the kitchen for a short break. "We really have to get busy preparing the black walnut and apple donuts," Maggie said.

"How come?" Ruby asked. "I didn't realize we'd put them on the official menu."

"I mean, I've had numerous requests for those donuts," Maggie said. "So many that I lost count."

"I've dealt with the same thing," Myra said.

"Me, too," Naomi said.

"Wait a minute," Ruby said. "Are you guys saying that people have been asking for those donuts we prepared for the book signing?"

"The very donuts you feature in your cookbook." Maggie smiled.

"Yeah, people really want more of those," Naomi said. "I almost made an entire batch yesterday."

"Why didn't you?" Myra asked. "I would have helped!"

"Why don't we whip some up now?" Maggie suggested. She watched Ruby out of the corner of her eye.

"I don't know, you guys," Ruby said.

"Why not?" Myra asked.

"Because," Ruby said. She was suddenly flushed. "A woman is dead."

"Yes," Maggie said. "She died, and it had nothing to do with you. Or with your recipes."

"I just wish I could remember if I really made that recipe up or not. Then maybe I wouldn't feel so responsible for all of this."

"You told me yourself that you searched high and low for any reference to the grandmother in all of your notes and archives," Maggie reminded her. "And you found nothing."

"That doesn't mean I didn't miss something," Ruby said. "Maybe I met the poor lady somewhere and forgot to give her credit. Maybe I got the recipe from some other relative after she died."

Maggie exhaled slowly. She had wanted to be careful about revealing what she had uncovered the night before. The last thing she wanted to do was to throw her normally rock-solid steady best friend into another emotional spiral.

"Ruby, you need to listen to me," Maggie began. "There's something I have to tell you."

"Oh no. What happened now?" Ruby asked.

"I did a little looking around online, and I found out that Laura Beth Swenson is not dead. She's living in a nursing home in Poplar Bluff."

"Wait a minute," Naomi asked. "Are you saying that after all that fuss was raised about a dead woman's recipes, it turns out she isn't even dead?"

"That's what I'm saying," Maggie said.

"When did you plan to tell me about this?" Ruby asked.

"I don't know," Maggie said. "To be honest, I wasn't sure when I was going to say anything. I didn't want to upset you even more."

"Did you think that keeping things from me was going to help?" Ruby challenged her. "It doesn't upset me one bit to find this out. As a matter of fact, it makes me feel like a weight has been lifted off my shoulders."

"What difference does it make whether she's dead or alive?" Myra asked. "These people are still accusing you of something."

Ruby smiled. "It makes all the difference in the world," she said. The color seemed to come back into her face and her eyes brightened as she spoke. "Now I know without a doubt that I didn't inadvertently plagiarize anything. And I know that because she's still alive."

"I still don't get it," Myra said.

"If she was dead, there was still a chance that I may have heard the recipe from her or something along those lines," Ruby explained. "But knowing she's still alive means that I would have absolutely had to have obtained permission to reprint her recipe if I had included it. I've always been a stickler for those details and so was my last editor. The thing is, I've been using a different editor for the past couple of years. It's not like I could have gone back and asked her to help me remember, but I do know that I never would have used the recipe of someone still living without them signing a waiver giving me permission."

"If I had realized that, I would have told you about her first thing when I got here this morning," Maggie said. "I'm sorry I waited."

"I understand your reasoning, and I'm the first to admit that I've not been myself the past few days. I guess I understand why you were cautious."

"Does this mean life will go back to normal around here now?" Orson asked, poking his head into the kitchen.

"What does that even mean?" Naomi asked. "What is normal around here anyway?"

Myra laughed. "I don't know about normal, but I do think this information could help figure out who murdered Sarah Beth. This could be a good place to start."

"You might be right," Ruby admitted. "Maybe we should go talk to her."

"Laura Beth?" Maggie asked. "You think?"

"I do, actually," Ruby said. "As a matter of fact, Naomi and Myra, would you two be willing to handle things around here after lunch?"

Naomi glanced at Myra. "Sure, we can handle things," she said. "Right, Myra?"

"Of course we can," Myra said. "What are you planning to do?"

"Well, I think Maggie and I might be in for a road trip," Ruby said. "How far is it to Poplar Bluff, anyway?"

"I don't know how I feel about this trip," Brett said a short time later. Maggie called him just before lunchtime to clue him in on her plans to head west with Ruby.

"It's just a road trip, Brett," Maggie said. "I am riding along with Ruby, so she doesn't go alone."

"I understand, but there's still a murder investigation happening," he said.

"Which you have clearly said she isn't a suspect for, right?"

"Yes, I have," Brett said. "There is no way Ruby could have had anything to do with Sarah Beth Swenson's death."

"There shouldn't be any problem with us going to see this woman, then," Maggie said.

"No, I suppose there isn't," Brett said. "Just try to keep everything low key, please. If the state police actually do wind up stepping in here and taking over this investigation, I really don't want there to be any red flags."

"Understood," Maggie said. "No table dancing at the nursing home."

"Very funny," Brett said, not amused. "Just be careful. Promise me that."

Maggie did her best to convince him that the trip would be straightforward. She planned to drive, since her car was much better on gas mileage, but agreed that Ruby would take over driving at some point.

"Are you ready?" Ruby said when she returned to the kitchen after placing the call to Brett.

"As ready as I'm ever going to be, I guess," Maggie said.

CHAPTER NINE

The trip to Poplar Bluff was just over three hours. Maggie drove most of the way, until they pulled over for a restroom break just west of Van Buren. Ruby offered to take over, and Maggie was in no mood to argue with her.

"Do you really think the state police are going to come in and take over the investigation?" Ruby asked.

"Honestly, I don't know," Maggie said. "Part of me hopes they do. Maybe an outside source will be able to step in and make better sense of the facts and evidence. I still don't know where this is going."

"You don't think there are any other suspects?" Ruby asked.

Maggie shook her head. "Not as far as I know," she said. "But the possibilities are wide open. It was most likely a random act of violence. I'm sure they'll figure out someone attacked her on the highway for some reason or another."

"It has to be," Ruby said. "Otherwise, it doesn't make a whole lot of sense."

"I feel bad for the other two, Heather and Liz," Maggie said. "I mean, they did lose a family member, and that has to be very difficult."

"Of course it is," Ruby said. "That's one reason I think this hit me so hard. I hate the thought that I might have caused someone pain. If I had ever been in contact with their grandmother or anyone else in their family, I wanted to know. I scoured my notes to find out. I had to be able to look at myself in the mirror."

"Ruby, if anything like this ever happens again, promise me you won't shut down like that," Maggie said. "And definitely don't shut me out. I'm here for you no matter what."

Ruby tapped the steering wheel with her fingers as she drove. "I will do my best to never do that again," she promised. "As long as you promise to keep me in the loop when you're going off to investigate another crime."

"I think we can make that compromise."

"You know, setting aside the tragedy of the poor woman's death, I really resent the intrusion of those women in my life," Ruby said.

"I don't blame you for one second," Maggie said. "Besides, those are some very angry women."

"I thought it was just Sarah Beth who felt that way," Ruby said.

"She certainly was pretty angry, but so were her sister and her niece. I found both of them to be a little insufferable and snarky."

"I wonder if Laura Beth will be the same?"

"I guess we're about to find out," Maggie said. She pointed out the window. "There's the nursing home."

Ruby parked the car close to the entrance.

"We're here to see Laura Beth Swenson," Maggie told the attendant at the desk just inside the front door.

"She's down the hall, last room on the right." The young man behind the desk barely looked at the two of them.

Maggie thanked him and headed down the hall. Ruby walked along beside her, suddenly quiet. "Are you okay?" Maggie whispered as they walked.

"Yeah, yeah," Ruby said. "I'm okay. Just hopeful I don't hear something I don't want to hear."

"I understand," Maggie said. "Why don't you let me do the talking?"

"That's alright," Ruby said. "It makes more sense for me to open the conversation, don't you think? After all, I'm the one who wants to make sure I haven't inadvertently plagiarized her recipes."

"Good cover story," Maggie mumbled as they approached the door. She almost kicked herself for not coming up with a strategy before they arrived. How else was she going to break the ice with the woman?

Ruby reached out and knocked on the door.

"Come in," a wavering voice called from the other side.

Ruby slowly pushed the door open, and Maggie followed her inside. A small woman was seated in a wingback chair on the opposite side of the room, almost completely camouflaged by the multicolored crocheted throw over her lap. Maggie was surprised to see someone of such advanced age, but when she added up the years between Heather and her great-grandmother, it made sense.

"Mrs. Swenson," Ruby called carefully.

"That's me," the woman said. Her voice was thick

and raspy. She coughed for a spell, then settled down. "Who's asking?"

"Well, ma'am, my name is Ruby Cobb, and this is my best friend, Maggie Mission."

"Pleasure to meet you," Laura Beth said. "Forgive me if I don't get up."

"Oh, that's alright," Maggie said.

"Now, tell me what you're here for," Laura Beth said. "But I will have to warn you. I already found God and I am not interested in life insurance. At my age it's sort of a moot point by now."

Ruby chuckled. Maggie could feel her relax a little. "We're not from a church," she said. "And I have never once been an insurance salesperson."

"In that case, forgive me for being so blunt, but why are you here?" Laura Beth asked. "These days, there just isn't any time to mess around with niceties and small talk."

"Well, this is going to sound strange, but have we ever met? Do you recognize me at all?" Ruby asked.

The older woman sat forward in her chair and studied Ruby. She looked her up and down and furrowed her brow for a moment before she answered.

"I don't think I have ever set eyes on you one

minute in my life," she said. "Are you some long lost kid of mine, or something?"

"Do you have any missing grandkids?" Ruby asked.

"Do you have a missing grandparent?" Laura Beth shot back.

"You certainly are in charge of all of your faculties." Maggie chuckled.

"Oh, honey," Laura Beth said. "I'm still as sharp as a tack. It's my legs and my balance that keep me here. To answer your previous question, I do have missing grandkids. Two of them. I am the grandmother of two women who haven't been around to see me in over three years."

"Your granddaughters don't come and see you?" Maggie asked.

Laura Beth shook her head. "Although from what I hear, only one of them is really to blame," she said. "Sarah Beth hasn't had anything to do with the family for years."

"So, you have no recollection of the two of us meeting ever?" Ruby said, pressing the older woman.

"No, not ever," Laura Beth said. "But now you have my curiosity going. Who are you, and why would we have met?"

Ruby exhaled slowly and shook her head. "Can

you explain, please?" she said to Maggie. "I need a moment."

"Sure," Maggie said. She turned to the older woman. "Ruby here is the author of numerous cookbooks. She is a bestseller, to be honest. Anyway, someone recently accused her of copying your recipes, and while she doesn't make a habit of plagiarism, she wanted to make sure if the two of you had ever met."

"You write cookbooks, and someone accused you of stealing a recipe from me?" Her eyes widened as she spoke, then promptly began coughing. Although it was difficult to differentiate between her laughter and the coughing fit.

"What is so funny?" Ruby asked, speaking up at last.

"It's just that I have never been what you would call a cook," Laura Beth said. "In fact, if I could pay someone to do it for me, I did."

"What about baking?" Ruby asked.

More raspy laughter. "Baking? Like pies and cakes and cookies? Not in this lifetime," Laura Beth said. "I wasn't much around the kitchen. It pains me to think you two traveled here to ask me these questions, and like I said, I'm not in here because my brain is oatmeal. This isn't a memory unit, you know. I think I would remember if I had recipes to steal."

Maggie and Ruby stared at each other for a moment. "Well, that's interesting," Ruby said.

"So, was it my granddaughter Liz who claimed you stole my nonexistent recipes?" Laura Beth asked. "Or her daughter, Heather?"

"Ma'am?" Ruby said, taken aback.

"It's alright," Laura Beth said, waving her hand in the air. "My grandchildren have never failed to disappoint me with their antics. Liz, for one thing, has never met a scandal or a scheme she could pass up. I'm afraid her daughter is cut from the same cloth. That's one reason they don't come around to visit me."

"Because they enjoy scamming people and don't want you to call them on it?" Maggie asked.

"Because they did it to me," Laura Beth said. "At least, Liz and her daughter have done it. I had to fight for control of my own checkbook for a little while. They were able to take me for about ten thousand dollars before I caught on. Their mother passed on many years ago. I can only imagine how they would treat her if she was still around. Poor Sarah Beth was smart enough to get away from their mess years ago. I think it hurt her pretty badly to remove them from her life, but it was the smartest thing she could have done, no matter how badly she might have missed them."

"That's terrible," Ruby breathed.

"It is. It's an awful thing," Laura Beth said. "So, tell me, how much did they take you for?"

CHAPTER TEN

"I'm not unhappy to be headed back," Ruby admitted in the car an hour later. They left the nursing home after a brief twenty-minute visit with the elderly woman.

"How old do you think she was?" Maggie asked as she drove west down the highway.

"Oh, likely she was in her mid-nineties," Ruby said. "I guess she would have to be for Heather to be her great-granddaughter."

"Right, that's true," Maggie said. "I'm wondering if we did the right thing."

"The right thing? You probably should have considered that before we left to come all the way to Poplar Bluff," Ruby said.

"Not that right thing," Maggie said. "The one

about not telling her that her granddaughter, Sarah Beth, had passed away."

"I don't think it was our place to tell her," Ruby said after a moment. "If she was going to hear that from someone, it shouldn't be from two perfect strangers trying to unravel what her other grand-daughters are up to."

Maggie sighed and switched lanes. "I guess you're right," she said. "Part of me feels like a jerk, though."

"What do you think she meant about Sarah Beth?" Ruby asked a short time later.

"I'm betting they scammed her at one point too, and she removed herself from the situation and stopped talking to them. I wonder if the reason they were with her this time was because of another scam?"

Ruby frowned. "You could be right. If they hadn't spoken in years, it would make sense that Liz and Heather lured her here for some reason."

"Wait a second," Maggie hesitated. "You said you'd been hearing from Sarah Beth for quite a while, right?"

"For some time, yes," Ruby said. "But she never accused me of anything until she arrived at the book signing. She mentioned our recipes being similar but that was meant about her own recipes, not anyone else's. She seemed excited about having recipes similar to mine, not upset."

"I guess it's possible that she conceived that idea on her way here from her home to Dogwood Mountain," Maggie mused. "Did you ever get the idea that something was off with her?"

"Not really," Ruby said. "She was a fan like the rest of the people who contacted me. I guess the only difference was that she wrote me over and over. It wasn't just a one-time thing. Why are you asking?"

Maggie sighed. "I don't know. I guess none of this has anything to do with her being killed by some random stranger. I'm just thinking out loud and hoping I come up with something helpful."

When they arrived back home in Dogwood Mountain, Maggie dropped Ruby off at her truck and drove the short distance to her home. Brett greeted her with a cup of tea the second she walked through the back door into the kitchen.

"Maybe I should look for a different job working at night," she joked. "I think I like this treatment."

"Donuts at night? That might take some time to catch on," he said. "How was your trip?"

"Good. Interesting," Maggie said. "Turns out it's true."

"What's that?" Brett asked.

"That was Sarah Beth and Liz's grandmother," Maggie said. "And it seems that there's a lot more to the truth then we ever thought."

"I made you tea. Don't keep me in suspense," Brett said.

"That whole story about their grandmother's recipes? It was all fiction," Maggie said. "The woman was not a cook. She said that if she was able to farm out the chore of cooking, that's what she did."

"Are you serious? So there never was a book of her recipes?" Brett asked. "What did we find in Sarah Beth's car then?"

"I think that's probably a question you'll have to ask the other two," Maggie said.

"I wish I had known that when I had another conversation with them," Brett said.

"You had another interview?"

Brett nodded. "I had another strange interview, yes," he said. "Liz is really pushing for the state police to get involved, but it seems she hasn't made the call yet."

"What about Heather? Is she still acting reluctant?" Maggie asked.

"Surprisingly, yes," Brett sad. "I really wish I could understand why."

"From what their grandmother said, it sounds like there was a lot of turmoil in their family," Maggie told him.

"Turmoil like what, exactly?" Brett asked.

"She wasn't specific, other than to say that none of her grandchildren have been to visit her in recent years," Maggie said. "She indicated that Sarah Beth didn't really speak to any of them, and that Liz and her daughter were known to scam and swindle people."

"Scam and swindle people? Their own grandmother said this?" Brett asked.

Maggie nodded quickly. "As a matter of fact, she asked Ruby how much they took her for," Maggie said.

"What did she say when you told her about Sarah Beth?" Brett asked quietly.

"We didn't say a word about that," Maggie said. "Honestly, I'm surprised you asked. In no way was it our place to tell her that her granddaughter was just murdered."

"We're still no closer to figuring out who killed the poor woman, though," Brett said. "As interesting as all of this new information you have might be, it still doesn't solve a murder."

"No, but it might explain it," Maggie said.

"How so? What do you mean?"

Maggie took a long swig of her tea, which had just cooled enough for her to drink. "Heather said they knew about Sarah Beth's love for Ruby's work. She said they invited her for the trip to be nice, but if the grandmother says they haven't spoken in years, maybe all of this was just another scam."

"You mean they were scamming Sarah Beth and Ruby was involved by default?"

Maggie shook her head. "I have no idea," she said. "At least, not yet."

CHAPTER ELEVEN

Maggie was groggy when she rose for work the following morning. She sent Brett off to work early and headed into the donut shop herself, eager to see Ruby. Although they had been together for hours the night before, she was looking forward to sharing what she had learned from Brett and his conversation with Heather and her mother.

Maggie had suggested that Brett call in the state police himself. That way, there would be less trouble with the Swenson family believing no one was taking the investigation seriously, but also, it was possible they'd be able to find something that Brett had missed.

She didn't know if it would make a difference, and part of her worried that the state police would have an issue with Brett's connection to Ruby. The same fear loomed over Brooks as chief of police in Dogwood Mountain. However, she had to trust her visit to the matriarch of the Swenson family. If even she was willing to share that the younger generations in her family weren't all that trustworthy, it had to mean something.

"How did you sleep last night?" Ruby asked her the second she walked through the back door.

"Apparently not as well as you did," Maggie said. "I'm surprised to see you here before I am."

"Let's just say I had a better, more restful night's sleep than I've had in a week," Ruby said. "I think it was a relief to go see Laura Beth and hear her explain what she did."

"I felt the same way. Knowing what we do about her granddaughters makes me feel a little better, too."

Ruby shook her head. "No, about the alleged recipe book that I had somehow plagiarized," she said. "I don't even think I realized how much that was bothering me. Not until I heard the truth."

Maggie nodded and tied her apron around her waist. "I wish we were closer to the truth about what happened to Sarah Beth," she said.

"I've been thinking about her quite a bit since we left Poplar Bluff," Ruby admitted. "I've been very worried about myself through all of this, failing to remember that a woman lost her life."

"Hopefully we can find some answers soon," Maggie said.

"Do you still plan to keep looking into this?" Ruby asked. "I mean, I understand that you were trying to protect me, and I really appreciate that. I figured that was the reason you agreed to go all the way to the other side of this state to visit Laura Beth."

"I do plan to continue to look into this," Maggie said. "Not that my husband isn't perfectly capable of figuring things out on his own, but I think he's just as lost as we are. And I don't think you should be hard on yourself one bit about getting to the bottom of the accusations made against you. I don't think either one of us has forgotten about the woman who was found dead."

Ruby smiled and returned to her work at the prep table. Maggie headed to the storage room and pulled out her supplies for the yeast donut varieties she planned to get started. Despite being offered a late start, Naomi and Myra both insisted that they would be in on their normal schedules. When she arrived, Naomi would start in on the other donut varieties for the day, including the black walnut and apple donuts Ruby had debuted for her book signing.

"You better set aside a half-dozen of those for Orson," Myra said while the first batch of the new donut variety cooled on the racks.

"Is he already here?" Maggie asked.

Myra nodded. "He's here and he's demanding a plate of those things," she said. "In fact, the entire dining room is pretty packed. I better get back out there and wait on a few more people before the line winds up going out the front doors." She rushed back to the dining room.

"Wow," Maggie said. "If she is that busy out there, I think I'll give her a hand. These scones can wait a while." She picked up a clean towel and placed it gingerly over the scone dough. She untied her soiled apron and headed out behind Myra.

When she emerged on the other side of the swinging door, Maggie nearly came face to face with Liz Swenson. "What are you doing here?" she asked as soon as she spotted her. Heather stood next to her in front of the display case.

"I want to talk to you," Liz seethed. "Now. You and your business partner."

"I'm afraid you need to get in line behind everyone else," Maggie said. "As you can see, we are rather busy this morning."

Liz shook her head. "I'm not here to order donuts

from you," she said. She glanced down at the display case. "Although I can see you've wasted no time in serving those donuts our grandmother invented."

"I can see your perspective has changed," Orson said behind the woman. Maggie looked over her shoulder at the older man who was carrying an empty coffee mug up to the counter for a refill. "The last I heard, it was your sister who was making those allegations against Ruby. Now it's you two, as well?"

"My sister," Liz said. "How dare you even mention her! She was murdered."

"I am aware," Orson said. "And so is everyone else."

"What are you doing here?" Maggie asked.

"I came here to ask you why you decided to go visit our grandmother," Liz said.

"The grandmother you all claimed was dead? I think that's my business," Maggie said, surprised they even knew about it.

"I'm sure you can understand why my mother is concerned about what you're up to," Heather spoke up and said. She moved next to Liz in front of the display case. "And it wasn't either of us who made the claims against your friend."

"You mean my business partner? Ruby isn't just my friend," Maggie said.

"Okay, fine, your business partner," Liz interrupted. "Why did you travel to Poplar Bluff and speak with my grandmother? What on earth were you doing there?"

"Getting to the bottom of the ridiculous claims your family made against my friend and business partner," Maggie said, emphasizing the last words.

"You didn't tell her about Aunt Sarah?" Heather said, her face going completely ashen.

"Of course not," Maggie said. "Unlike some people, I'm not determined to be cruel."

"Determined to be cruel? What on earth do you mean by that?" Liz asked. "I don't care what that old lady told you, neither of us is cruel."

"It wasn't your grandmother I was speaking about," Maggie said. She heard the swinging door open behind her and was aware that Ruby and Naomi were both standing there. "If I was going to talk to you about your cruelty, I would start with your sister, not your grandmother."

"My sister," Liz said, clearly shocked by the accusation. "I don't know whether to reach across this counter and slap you for saying that or wait to hear what you mean. Because it better be something good."

Maggie looked over her shoulder at Ruby. "How

long ago was it you said Sarah Beth messaged you the first time, Ruby?" she asked. "I mean before the other day when she showed up here for your book signing."

"A couple of years, at least," Ruby said. "She started writing to me after my last book was published."

Maggie turned her attention back to Liz and Heather. "And the three of you, you were staying at the Dogwood House, correct?"

"Yeah, but what does that have to do with anything?" Liz asked. "That's the only bed and breakfast in this town."

"You're right about that," Maggie said. "Which is how I know your trip had to be planned ahead of time."

"That still doesn't explain what on earth you're talking about," Liz snapped.

"As you said, your sister was a big fan of Ruby's. You two found that out and decided to bring her here to cause trouble. She wasn't on speaking terms with either of you, but you knew that you could use something she loved as a way to lure her back in to your lives."

"What does that have to do with anything?" Liz asked. "We missed her and thought if she knew Ruby would be here, she would come with us. We were just trying to do something nice."

"Ruby, when did you first hear about Sarah Beth's allegations against you and her grandmother's recipes?" Maggie asked. By now, the entire dining room had gone quiet. All eyes were on the front counter where Maggie stood in front of the two women.

"I never heard a word about it until the other day when she started shouting those allegations at me from the back of the line," Ruby said. "And it was the first day I met the two of them, as well."

"To me, it sounds like you put the idea into Sarah Beth's head that her beloved Ruby had stolen from your grandmother. Until she was with the two of you, she didn't have a single bad thing to say about Ruby, did she? How cruel is it that you put an idea like that in her head? She loved Ruby's work, and you created a problem that never even existed."

"What never even existed?" Orson asked.

"For one thing, Laura Beth Swenson was not your late grandmother," Maggie said. "Turns out she's very much alive. And the funny thing is, the woman never considered herself a cook, let alone someone who would collect her own recipes."

"Again, what does that have to do with anything?" Liz asked.

"I just find the timing of all this very odd. It's pretty convenient that you had a way to get your sister to talk to you again, and instead of letting her enjoy meeting an author she likes, you decide it's better to use her as part of your games. You didn't miss her at all. You just needed her to be a pawn."

"This is so confusing. You two ladies tricked a family member into thinking you cared about her?" Orson asked, his arms crossed.

"It is rather confusing," Ruby spoke up. "In all the years Sarah Beth wrote to me, she never once made any kind of accusation against me. If anything, she was lonely. However, I guess I'd rather be lonely than be involved with the two of you."

"Your grandmother had a lot to say," Maggie said. "The first thing she asked Ruby was how much money you got from her. According to her, the two of you are quite the scam artists. This all makes perfect sense. I think it's time to stop denying things."

"Mom, I think it's best we leave now," Heather said. She pulled on her mother's arm.

Liz shook her daughter off and stared at Maggie. "No, I think I want to hear more about this," she said. "Where do you get off saying anything about my daughter and me when your husband is the one running a circus around here? Why do you think we suggested calling in another set of cops? I could only imagine what you have to hide from them."

"I don't have anything to hide from anyone," Maggie said. "Neither does my husband. What about you, Ruby? Anything to hide?"

"Not a single thing," Ruby said.

"When are they supposed to be here, anyway?" Maggie asked. "You did make that phone call, didn't you? Heather, I believe you were the one that was going to call them."

"Of course, she did," Liz snapped. She looked at her daughter.

"Well, did you or did you not call them?" Orson demanded.

"I don't have to answer your questions, old man," Heather said.

"Did you make a phone call?" Liz asked quietly. "Heather, did you call them or not?"

"Mom, I don't want to talk about this right now," she said. "Come on. Let's get out of here."

"Maybe you should listen to your daughter," Maggie said. "And when you two are alone, you should ask her why she's so reluctant to call the state police in the first place. It makes me wonder if she has something to hide."

"What would she have to hide?" Liz asked. "It seems to me that you all are the ones with the secrets."

"We don't have any secrets around here," Ruby said. "That's what we've been trying to tell you all along."

"She's right," Myra said. "You can call in the FBI for all we care. You can have them come down here and look over my husband's shoulder as well if you'd like. Just because we are married to members of law enforcement, doesn't mean we're guilty of anything."

"Well, just because we're reluctant to believe you, doesn't mean we are," Liz said.

"I'm not so sure about that," Maggie said, gazing at Heather. "I think one of you is hiding something from the other. Right, Heather?"

"I don't have to answer you," she said. "Mom, if you're not ready to go, I'm just going to leave you here."

"What do you think my daughter has to hide from me?" Liz asked.

Maggie cleared her throat. "Look, if the two of you were in on some scam where you thought you were going to extort money out of my best friend, that's one thing," she said. "But if you deliberately manipulated your sister into being part of that, that's outright disgusting."

"Those are some pretty tall accusations," Liz said.

"If you don't like that one, you're not going to like what else is coming out of her mouth," Orson said.

"What is he talking about?" Liz asked.

"He's probably talking about the fact that I find it rather suspicious that Heather is so reluctant to have the state police come in and look at things," Maggie said. "That makes me think she has a lot more to hide than you do."

"Meaning what?" Liz asked.

"Meaning your daughter killed your sister, lady," Orson said. "Even I picked up on that one and I sit at the Old Timer's table."

Before Liz could react, Heather rushed through the front door and ran out into the parking lot. She was stopped by Brooks on his way in for his morning cup of coffee. He held out his hand and began asking questions.

"I don't understand," Liz said. "Why do you think my daughter killed my sister?"

"For the same reason you're not screaming at me

that she didn't do it," Maggie said flatly. "You have your suspicions, the same as we do."

"It took about five minutes of her sitting in the back of Brooks's police car for her to make a full confession," Brett told Maggie after lunch. They were seated together in the far booth close to the bathrooms.

"What was her motive?" Maggie asked. She had suspected Heather was the killer, but the reasons eluded her.

"Her aunt found out what was going on," Brett explained.

"She said the idea to try to extort money from Ruby was both hers and her mother's, but Liz had no idea that it was Heather who murdered her sister."

"I hate to ask, but why was the car out on the highway?" Maggie asked.

"Because Heather left it there, and she planted the fake book of recipes along with the copy of Ruby's new cookbook."

"But she was able to get her there and back to the Dogwood House without arousing her mother's suspicions," Maggie said. "I'm not sure I know how that happened."

"I wasn't sure at first either, but we found a ride share app on her phone with proof that she called them. Apparently, she told her mother she was going out for a run, ended up meeting her aunt, doing the deed, and then called for a ride back to the Dogwood House."

"She probably tricked her aunt into meeting her," Maggie said. Her stomach turned over again considering another layer of the cruelty. "That poor woman very likely believed her family missed her. You know, when she stepped out of line and started yelling at my best friend, I found myself feeling all sorts of enraged at her."

"And now?"

"And now I just feel sad," she said. "I hate that she was manipulated by members of her own family. I can't imagine doing something like that to a person I love."

"It's all terrible," Brett agreed. "I hate what it did to Ruby's confidence." He looked past the counter. "This was a rough ride for her."

"Yes, it was," Maggie said. "But it was also a confidence booster. She told me after Liz left with Brooks and Heather that she was forced to examine a few things. That made her much more certain that she is where she wants to be in her life."

"That's a wonderful feeling," Brett said, taking his wife's hand in his own.

"Get a room, you two," Orson said from his seat near the window.

"We have a room," Maggie said, without pulling her eyes away from Brett. "And a house, and a business."

"Yeah, well, you don't have to keep reminding the rest of us that you two are still newlyweds," Orson grumbled.

AUTHOR'S NOTE

I'd love to hear your thoughts on my books, the storylines, and anything else that you'd like to comment on—reader feedback is very important to me. My contact information, along with some other helpful links, is listed on the next page. If you'd like to be on my list of "folks to contact" with updates, release and sales notifications, etc.... just shoot me an email and let me know. Thanks for reading!

Also...

... if you're looking for more great reads, Summer Prescott Books publishes several popular series by outstanding Cozy Mystery authors.

CONTACT SUMMER PRESCOTT BOOKS PUBLISHING

Blog and Book Catalog: http://summerprescottbooks.com

Email: summer.prescott.cozies@gmail.com

And…be sure to check out the Summer Prescott Cozy Mysteries fan page and Summer Prescott Books Publishing Page on Facebook – let's be friends!

To sign up for our fun and exciting newsletter, which will give you opportunities to win prizes and swag, enter contests, and be the first to know about New Releases, click here: http://summerprescottbooks.com

Made in United States
North Haven, CT
17 June 2023

37874991R00067